"Move over Snoopy. Pavlov is the funniest dog I have ever seen . . . he and his owner have more adventures in hilarity than should be legal."
—Ocala (Fla.) Star-Banner

"Martin's humor is as hilariously playful as his drawings and it's no wonder that he has developed a worldwide following."
—Pasadena Star-News

Ted Martin

A TOM DOHERTY ASSOCIATES BOOK

PAVLOV

A TOR Book

Published by Tom Doherty Associates, Inc.
49 West 24th Street
New York, NY 10010

ISBN: 0-812-57478-8   Can. ISBN: 0-812-57479-6

First Tor edition: August 1988

0 9 8 7 6 5 4 3 2 1

"Look, Ma! Pavlov's invented a sun-dial with glow-in-the-dark markings."

"Call a real estate office, quick! Pavlov
just dropped his Termite Farm Kit in the
basement."

"I've never heard of Dog's Day — I'll just have to take his word for it."

"Ah . . . the smell of freshly risen bread dough."

"Sit down. Your future don't look too good . . ."

"If you hadn't lost the carbon paper, you wouldn't have to type four copies of everything."

"Slow down . . . gasp . . . I can't . . .
puff . . . keep up with you . . ."

"I don't care if you don't like the food.
Don't let me catch you slipping it to the
dog."

"Mother's not crazy about your idea of having a phone in the car."

"What's a four-letter word for the outer covering of a tree?"

"They're not walnuts; they're snails!"

"This has gotta be harder than pedaling a bicycle made for two."

"Pavlov showed me an old book that said hens would lay if they sat on something hard and shiny . . ."

"I've got a bit of a problem here. Can you suck in your nose?"

"Bring on the steak, Mother. I've tucked
Pavlov into bed."

"As this is your first game, I'm gonna go
easy on you."

"Nobody leaves this room until I find
out where today's paper is."

"I'm gonna cry if that's the cake with
the file in it."

"I had the same problem with the return spring on my Murphy bed."

"Mother! Did you say there was some cherry cheese cake on top of the fridge?"

"Hold it, genius! What if a rescue ship appears in that direction?"

"And what have you guys been up to
while I've been shopping?"

"We gotta lose 10 pounds. Any suggestions?"

"Hey, buster! Get this dog a porterhouse
steak, and move it."

"ONE, please."

"We got any life-sized, rag-doll
mailmen?"

"Got any spray cans with less
propellant in them?"

"Mother! Call the paper and ask them
what's supposed to be on the back
page."

"Anybody seen my hairpiece?"

"I hate Blackjack! I wanna play Old Maid."

"He's rescuing the cat."

"The other way, dummy."

"You can confide in me, Mother; we're
the only ones in the room . . ."

"— and no cheating, OK?"

"This is your idea, so where are we gonna get five more dwarfs?"

"OK, ready when you are . . ."

"What's taking you so long defrosting
that freezer?"

"I could have sworn I heard that clock strike 'meow.'"

"He thought we'd get set up on a camp
site quicker if he starched and ironed the
tent."

"And just be extra careful where that hormonal plant food lands."

"Don't worry. Pavlov's too fat and
dumb to jump that high for roast beef."

"Cranberry jelly?"

"Can't figure out how your appointment cards got mixed up, but you needed that tooth out anyhow."

"Claims we had a power cut."

"Don't let Father catch you using his
fork-lift truck."

"Your hiccup cure is taking its time."

"Pavlov, my TV channels keep changing."

"Can't wait for your new way of
preparing meatballs and spaghetti,
Pavlov."

"Ha! Caught you moving your lips."

"Let me guess — is it potato soup?"

"Hold it! I've just thought of a new rule."

"Hot dog is a no-no word here."

"To be fair, Pavlov, this is the only way
you can play blindman's bluff."

"I'll raise you two hundred dollars and
see you . . ."

"Some garden — one carrot, one pea
and a tomato."

"According to this book on etiquette,
chicken is one of the foods that can be
eaten with the fingers."

"Beats me how you manage that
exercise so effortlessly."

"Are you aiming on winning that
retriever competition, Pavlov?"

"Don't be ridiculous, Mother. Why would a cat want to jump off a window ledge 50 feet from the ground?"

"The idea of the game is to try and outstare your opponent. The one who blinks first hands over 50 chocolate-chip cookies."

"I've told you enough times — it's rude
to watch people eat."

"We've nearly got a picture, Pavlov —
raise your left ear a bit."

"Here's a cookie for Polly."

"You put Tabasco sauce in the salad dressing!?"

"OK, you've got one minute to impress me."

"There's a message we've got a
stowaway on board."

"Next time I'm over for dinner, can we
eat out on the patio?"

"I'm getting tired — let's change places."

"Let me tie this, and then I'll give you
your first skateboard lesson."

"I told you it wasn't what you thought it
was."

"Look, Pavlov — no hands!"

"Pavlov took me to a Doggyware party."

"This is a toughie — four letters, one
syllable and sounds like tire . . ."

"Are you sure this is the way to play squash?"

"Admit it, Mother. Pavlov's a great
guard dog."

"Just like we guessed — another
dachshund."

"Who's the turkey who ordered a Milk-
Bone souffle?"

"Check the front door. I think the
mailman's been here."

"If you have to squeeze the toothpaste in the middle, Pavlov, don't do it with your mouth."

"Why don't you break down and buy
him a pair of boots?"

"Of course the chow mein was crunchy.
You ate the chopsticks."

"Isn't it amazing how this old boat has
held up over the years?"

"Breakfast!"

"Ever thought of catching it in your mouth?"

"I told you not to wash the sails."

"Ready when you are — and no cheating."

"Do I smell fresh popcorn? . . ."

"Pavlov, when you share my bath you
follow my rules . . . Pavlov?"

"Those tax guys aren't gonna go for
depreciation on a doghouse."

"Don't shout 'fore' until you've hit the ball!"

"We forgot to put the stamp on."

"Cut the astronaut game, Pavlov. I need
the sink plungers."

"Now here's another joke that'll really
slay ya."

"Well, aren't you going to wish me
happy birthday?"

"Will you quit hangin' around?"

"You the guys that need a typewriter
ribbon changed?"

"Don't slalom down Father, Pavlov, he's
had a hard day."

"Ten minutes of fishing and he gets
bored."

"Without moving my lips I will make it appear that Pavlov is saying 'Polly wants a cracker' . . ."

"Come on and try this bargain steak I just cooked."

"That doghouse has solar and wind
power, but Pavlov still has to rely on us
to keep him in dog biscuits."

"Every time Pavlov pricked up his ears
the auctioneer thought it was a bid."

"Nothing tastes better than a sneaky,
private, all-to-oneself midnight snack."

"Wanna slow down a bit?"

"Ease up on the duck call — I can hear footsteps."

"When's that dumb bird gonna learn to count the right way?"

"Anesthetic wear off, then?"

"The rules state you can build houses and hotels on your property — no doghouses."

"Y'know, privacy disappeared when
trampolines were invented."

"Can't guess what's for dinner, but it
sure smells good."

"Well, what are we waiting for?"

"Pavlov wants to know if that's one scoop or two for the new ornamental pool."

"C'mon, I'll show you what we learned
tonight — but stop grinning . . ."

"If you're sleepwalking toward that
chicken leg — I already ate it."

"Show me something that says the captain must go down with his ship."

"What are you doing back there with
your spaghetti?"

"The mailman bit you . . . ?"

"Pavlov's really on the ball. A snap of my fingers and he brings my slippers."

"He's found something wrong with the plumbing in the basement — and he won't tell me what."

"Wanna be a sport and raise your left arm for half an hour or so?"